Put Beginning Readers on the Right Track with
ALL ABOARD READING™

The All Aboard Reading series is especially for beginning readers. Written by noted authors and illustrated in full color, these are books that children really and truly *want* to read—books to excite their imagination, tickle their funny bone, expand their interests, and support their feelings. With four different reading levels, All Aboard Reading lets you choose which books are most appropriate for your children and their growing abilities.

Picture Readers—for Ages 3 to 6
Picture Readers have super-simple texts with many nouns appearing as rebus pictures. At the end of each book are 24 flash cards—on one side is the rebus picture; on the other side is the written-out word.

Level 1—for Preschool through First Grade Children
Level 1 books have very few lines per page, very large type, easy words, lots of repetition, and pictures with visual "cues" to help children figure out the words on the page.

Level 2—for First Grade to Third Grade Children
Level 2 books are printed in slightly smaller type than Level 1 books. The stories are more complex, but there is still lots of repetition in the text and many pictures. The sentences are quite simple and are broken up into short lines to make reading easier.

Level 3—for Second Grade through Third Grade Children
Level 3 books have considerably longer texts, use harder words and more complicated sentences.

All Aboard for happy reading!

For Jeri — G.H.

Special thanks to Tracy Lorraine Smith, Forecast Systems Laboratory, NOAA.

Photo credits: pp. 7, 10, 42, 45, and back cover, courtesy of National Severe Storms Laboratory; p. 48, courtesy of Leo Ainsworth/National Severe Storms Laboratory; pp. 17, 20-21, courtesy of American Red Cross; p. 29, Warren Faidley/Weatherstock; title page, courtesy of NASA.

Library of Congress Cataloging-in-Publication Data

Herman, Gail. 1959-
   Storm chasers / by Gail Herman : illustrated by Larry Schwinger.
      p.   cm. — (All aboard reading)
   Summary: Describes how tornadoes behave and how the meteorologists who track them work.
   1. Storms—Juvenile literature.   2. Tornadoes—Juvenile literature.   3. Meteorologists—Juvenile literature.   4. Weather forecasting—Juvenile literature.   5. Astronautics in meteorology—Juvenile literature.   [1. Tornadoes.   2. Weather forecasting.
3. Astronatuics in meteorology.]   I. Schwinger, Larry, ill.
II. Title.   III. Series.
QC941.3.H47   1997
551.55'3—dc21

                                                                    96-50239
                                                                         CIP
                                                                          AC

ISBN 0-448-41638-7 (GB) A   B   C   D   E   F   G   H   I   J

ISBN 0-448-41624-7 (pbk) A   B   C   D   E   F   G   H   I   J

ALL
ABOARD
READING™

Level 3
Grades 2-3

STORM CHASERS

Tracking Twisters

By Gail Herman
Illustrated by Larry Schwinger

With photographs

Grosset & Dunlap • New York

Tornado!

Wee-oh! Wee-oh! Sirens blare. People hurry to a radio or TV and quickly flick it on. Hearts racing, they hear the emergency weather report: "Tornado warning!"

Everywhere, people scurry for shelter. The tornado could hit at any minute. Water is left running. Refrigerators are left open.

Outside all is quiet. Dark, heavy clouds hang in the sky. It is hot. Sticky.

Suddenly, lightning flashes. Thunder booms. A sheet of rain pours down. A minute later, hailstones big as fists clatter to the ground. The wind grows fierce and wild.

The clouds become one giant thunderhead. A point stretches toward the ground.

The point grows longer, and wider. It is a funnel now. The cloud is shaped like an ice-cream cone, or cotton candy on a stick. But it is deadly.

The funnel is twisting. Lower, lower, lower it sinks.

The noise is earthshaking—like thousands of roller coasters bucking and roaring. Inside, in shelters and basements and closets, people cover their ears.

The storm gathers force. Lightning crackles all around. Houses shake. Cars rock.

The funnel spins to the ground. Now it is a huge cloud of twisting, roaring, buzzing dirt and dust—a tornado.

It crashes through houses. It shatters glass. It sweeps away everything it touches.

Trees are plucked right out of the ground. Trucks are tossed high into the air. Roofs are lifted. Buildings crumble. Beams and planks, bricks and furniture fly everywhere.

The tornado races along, smashing everything in its path. Suddenly, it rises. It passes over one block. Then another. House after house is spared. Then it touches down again leaving more homes destroyed. More buildings damaged.

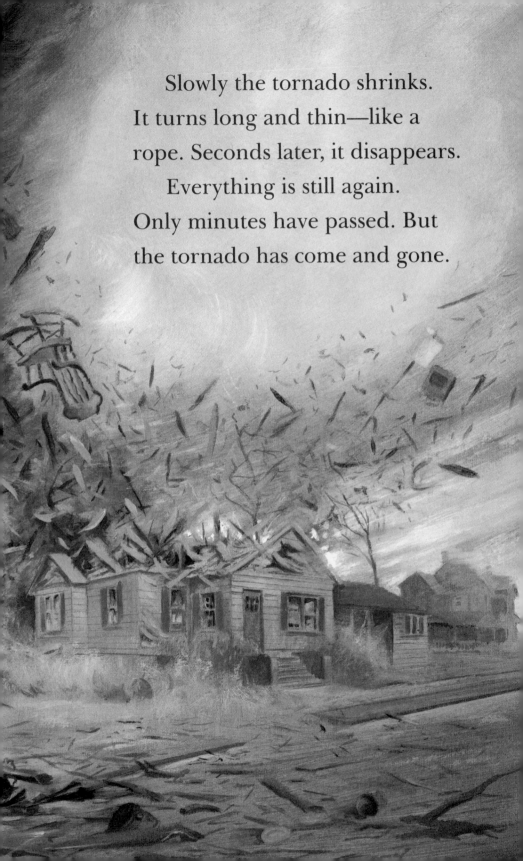

Slowly the tornado shrinks.
It turns long and thin—like a
rope. Seconds later, it disappears.
Everything is still again.
Only minutes have passed. But
the tornado has come and gone.

People come out from hiding. They crawl out from under piles of brick and wood and stone. They look around, dazed.

Houses are broken to bits and pieces. Cars are turned over. Dust and sand litter the ground. Street lights . . . signs . . . everything is ripped out of place, twisted and bent.

People are shocked and still afraid.

And they are lucky. They had time to hide. They had time to run.

But not everyone runs <u>from</u> a tornado. Some people run after them.

Who? Scientists who want to find out more about tornadoes. They want to learn how to tell where and when a tornado will strike. They want to give people more time to find safety.

Who else? Photographers who take pictures of storms. Reporters who are after a good story. People who are interested in weather and want to know more.

Who are these people?

Storm chasers.

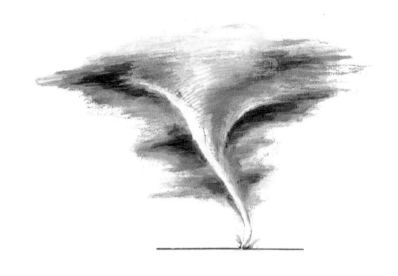

Ready for Anything

It's a Sunday in June. A storm chaser named Ross is on his way to the movies. This chaser is also a scientist. He studies weather, and he is called a meteorologist. (You say it like this: mee-tee-or-OL-oh-jist.)

The sky is overcast. It is hot.

Maybe there will be a thunderstorm, Ross thinks. Maybe even a tornado.

He reaches for his car phone. No movie for him. Instead, he calls his partner, Jill.

"Meet me at the weather station!" he tells her excitedly.

At the station, the two scientists pore over computer screens. They check weather information. Temperature. Wind readings.

Warm, damp air is moving up from Mexico. Cold, dry air is moving down from Canada.

Ross and Jill look at one another. If the cold and warm air collide, a tornado can happen.

CANADA

COLD

HOT

GULF OF MEXICO

How? When hot air meets cold air, the cold air slides underneath. The hot air rises. Drops of water are created. And giant thunder clouds form.

Sometimes the hot air gets trapped in the cloud. Sometimes it breaks through with a blast, and the cold air is sent into a whirl. Then a tornado <u>may</u> strike.

Jill and Ross can't be sure. Maybe they'll drive for miles and see nothing. In fact, that's what most chases amount to. But Jill and Ross are willing to take that chance.

The partners rush into a chase car. It is already packed. There are cameras to snap the tornado in action. Maps to help them track it. A laptop computer to get up-to-the-minute information from the weather service. And a tape recorder, so they can remember everything.

The storm chasers are ready for anything. Most of all, they are ready for a tornado.

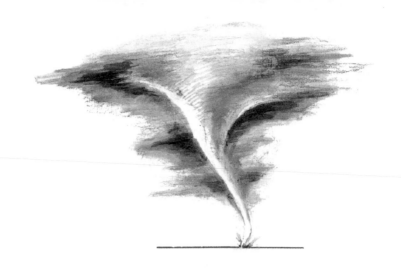

Tornado Power

Tornado. Twister. Cyclone. Three different names for the same powerful windstorm.

There are other kinds of storms.

Dust devils whirl up from sandy deserts. They are usually small and last only a minute or two.

Waterspouts are tornadoes that form over water. A strong one can pull the water up from a pond—and the fish, too!

Then there are hurricanes—powerful wind and rainstorms. Hurricanes begin over tropical seas. They build slowly over time and last for days and days. Trees are flattened. Buildings are washed away. People abandon their homes as neighborhoods and entire towns are flooded.

Hurricanes have their own chasers.
Hurricane hunters. These hunters risk
their lives every time they venture out
in a storm. Ninety of them have died.

Why?

They fly planes right into the center of
the hurricane. That is how they get
information. The center is calm and still.
But to get there, pilots have to pass
through wild winds of 70 to 100 miles an
hour.

Still, hurricane winds are not nearly as strong as tornado gusts. Tornadoes have the fastest, most dangerous winds on Earth—winds of more than 300 miles an hour!

Tornadoes are also dangerous for a different reason. They strike suddenly—and no one knows where they'll go or what they'll do.

A tornado may speed as fast as 70 miles per hour when it's on the ground. Or it may move slower than a turtle.

A tornado may travel hundreds of miles. Or just a few.

It may last hours. Or just a few seconds.

Sometimes tornadoes attack in groups.
One hundred and forty-eight tornadoes
struck on the very same day in April 1974.
Town after town in midwestern America
and Canada was wiped out. More than
three hundred people died. They were hit
by flying wreckage, buried under houses,
flung around by savage winds.

Students at a high school in Ohio were lucky that day. They'd been rehearsing a play on the auditorium stage. One girl glanced out the window and spotted the tornado. The students raced into the hallway, covering their heads. Seconds later, all the school buses blew right onstage.

A man in another town crawled under the couch in his living room. He held onto one couch leg with all his might. The tornado struck his house. Winds gusted all about. When the tornado moved on, the man looked up. He was still clutching that couch leg. But he was outside. There was no house. No furniture. And the rest of the couch had disappeared.

One woman hid in her bathtub. The
house flew apart around her. The tub
snapped out from the floor. The next
thing she knew, the tub turned into a sled.
And the woman was sliding into the
woods!

Strange things happen during tornadoes. Chickens are plucked clean by the wind. Houses are picked up and turned around—and not even glasses are broken. One man in Wichita, Kansas, was lifted up right into a tornado. He saw tires and a tractor whirling around him. Then he saw a bed—a bed neatly made up with the blanket still tucked in. If only he could reach it, he thought. It looked so comfortable!

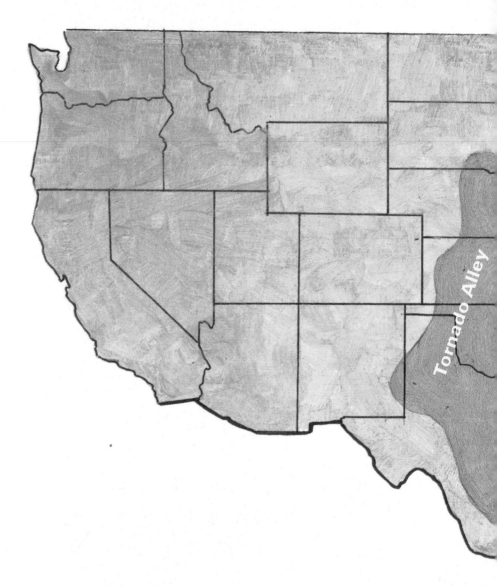

Tornado Alley

Tornadoes can be big ones or they can be small. About eight hundred tornadoes hit the United States each year. And they've struck all fifty states.

But most tornadoes hit Missouri,

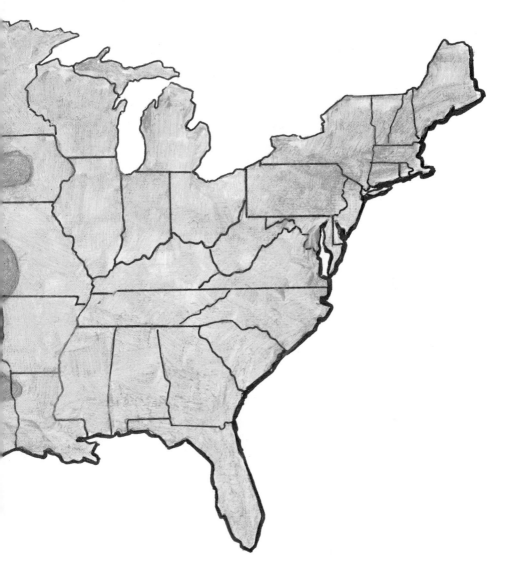

Kansas, Oklahoma, and Texas. This
stretch of land gets so many storms that
it is called Tornado Alley.

And Tornado Alley is where you'll find
storm chasers!

The Chase Is On!

Thunder booms overhead. The rain pours down, and Jill turns on the windshield wipers. The road is wet. Slick. She drives carefully.

She is thinking about another storm chaser. The one who died in a car accident, driving along these same rainsoaked highways.

Giant raindrops splatter on the roof. They run down the windows like waterfalls. Jill squints through the teeming rain. Lightning bolts blind her for seconds at a time. It is tough going.

Clank! Clink! Hailstones hit the car. Whoosh! Wind whistles through the windows. The car shakes, tossed by every gust.

"What should we do?" Ross cries above the noise.

"Find shelter!" Jill shouts.

Four large hailstones

Storm chasing is dangerous, and chasers are always careful. They don't want to be caught in the middle of a storm. They want to see the entire tornado.

"There's an overpass up ahead," Jill says. "I'll get us there."

But the car swerves on the slippery road. The scientist jams the brakes. The car spins. It lurches to a stop. Ross glances out the window.

"Oh no!" he cries. "The tornado!"

A quarter of a mile away . . . about five city blocks . . . the big swirling cloud of dust and dirt looms up.

The scientists are so close they can't see the top. They are so close they can't see the bottom. They just see something dark and big. Something turning, turning, turning.

Jill hits the gas. Ross looks for a ditch—someplace to take cover.

The black smoky column snakes farther away. It spins into the distance, out of sight.

The wind dies down. The shaking stops.

The scientists pull over.

"Whew!" says Ross. "That was close! We didn't even see it!"

The tornado loomed larger than a towering mountain! How could they have missed it? Easy. It was wrapped in rain.

The rain covered the twister like a blanket. So the chasers didn't see it—until they were almost in it.

Both scientists take deep breaths. They check their laptop for information. The storm is moving north. And so are they.

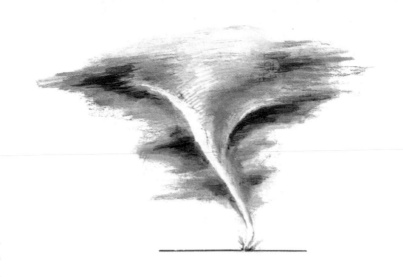

The Chasers

People have always chased storms. There were just a few chasers at first. They were drawn to storms—to their strange beauty and their force. They loved seeing nature at its most powerful.

They would roam the plains of the Midwest. They would go out in late spring, searching and searching.

These people weren't trained. They weren't even scientists. But they did take pictures. They took notes about clouds and temperatures. And when they saw a tornado form, they would call the sheriff or the police. They would start the warning.

Some scientists took notice. Maybe these storm chasers were onto something, they thought. So they went into the field too.

Scientists had lots of ideas. Could they fly a rocket into a tornado? Maybe a plane without any crew? No, they decided. Those ideas wouldn't work.

But they could try something else. They could try and place special instruments in the path of a tornado. These instruments could help them learn about tornadoes close up.

First scientists tried TOTO. TOTO was an invention named after the dog in "The Wizard of Oz." But this TOTO was a weather station. It looked like a giant garbage can. And it weighed 400 pounds.

Scientists had to carry TOTO to the storm in a pickup truck. Then five people had to haul it out. TOTO was that heavy. In fact, TOTO was <u>too</u> heavy. It took too much time to set up. And the tornado could close in at any second. So scientists came up with another invention—Turtles.

Turtles are small flat packages loaded with instruments. They are much easier to set up than TOTO.

Turtles are what scientists used in their latest project: VORTEX. In 1994 and 1995, science teams combed Oklahoma, Texas, and Kansas looking for tornadoes. They piled into vans and cars with rooftop weather stations.

Pilots jumped into planes. They followed the storm. Their job? To help out the ground crews. How big was the tornado? How fast was it moving? From way up high, they could answer these questions.

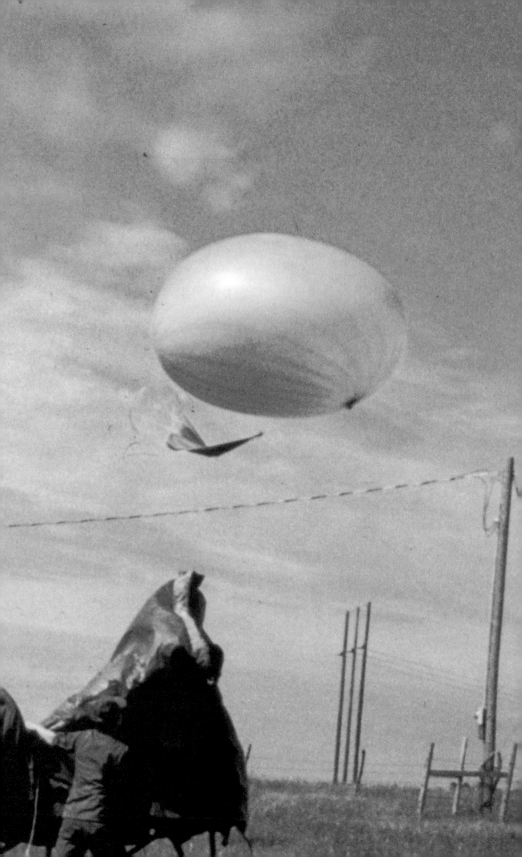

Scientists let loose huge balloons—balloons with measuring instruments dangling from them. Whoosh! Up they would fly. They would be tossed by heavy winds and carried higher and higher still. Then, pop! The balloons would burst. Parachutes would open, and carry the instruments to Earth.

These instruments told scientists about the air and temperature way up high. And the balloons also told scientists about wind speed and direction.

Scientists learned a lot from each tornado they tracked. But more work needs to be done. Tornadoes are still a mystery. A mystery that needs to be solved.

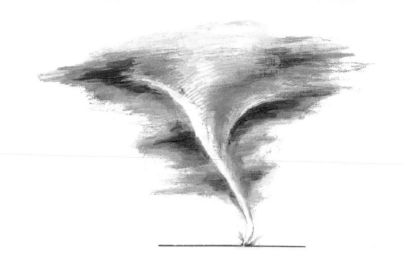

When a Tornado Hits

You're listening to the radio. Suddenly you hear the news. There's a severe storm heading your way. It's a tornado watch!

You run to the window. The skies are dark. It starts to rain. Thunder booms in the distance. The clouds hang low. A funnel seems to form.

What do you do?

You keep listening . . . to the radio or TV, whether you're at home or at school. It is important to know if the tornado watch changes into a tornado warning.

That means a tornado has actually been spotted. Or radar has picked it up for certain.

Don't use the telephone. There is lots and lots of lightning and electricity during these storms. You could get a shock from the wires.

If you are home, go to the basement. Get under the stairs or a piece of heavy furniture.

What if you don't have a basement? Get in a closet in the middle of your home. Kneel on the floor facing a wall. Put your hands over your head.

At school, stay away from gyms and auditoriums. Big rooms like these can collapse in an instant.

If you are outside, find a hiding place that is lower than the ground. A ditch or a hole would be good. Then lie down and cover your head.

If you are in a car, get out. It is hard to drive faster than a tornado. Again, take cover in a ditch.

And if you ever think of chasing a
tornado—or any kind of storm—think
again. Only experts should go storm
chasing.

Remember, a tornado may be exciting.
But its power can destroy homes and lives.